Newbery and Brahms' Lullaby by Johannes Brahms ᔓ THE MOON ᔓ Around the Moon by Jules Verne ᔓ THE WORLD ᔓ The Wonderful Wizard of Oz by L. Frank Baum, The Wind in the Willows by Kenneth Grahame, Li
ark Twain, A Christmas Carol by Charles Dickens, Moby-Dick by Herman Melville, The Secret Garden by Frances Hodgson Burnett, Heidi by Johanna Spyri, Black Beauty b ... and His K
Count of Monte Cristo by Alexandre Dumas, Kidnapped by Robert Louis Stevenson, Gulliver's Travels by Jonathan Swift and Twenty Thousand Leagues Under the Sea by ... ls by Jona
Wonderland by Lewis Carroll ᔓ THE MOUNTAINS ᔓ Peter Pan and Wendy by J.M. Barrie ᔓ THE CAVE ᔓ Treasure Island by Robert Louis Stevenson and Kidnapped ... Little Red
mm and Wilhelm Grimm, Snow-White and Rose-Red as told by Jacob Grimm and Wilhelm Grimm, Beauty and the Beast by Jeanne-Marie Leprince de Beaumont and Rapunzel as told by Jacob Grimm and Wilhelm Grimm ᔓ THE
yan, Twinkle, Twinkle, Little Star by Jane Taylor, Hush-a-Bye Baby as adapted by John Newbery and Brahms' Lullaby by Johannes Brahms ᔓ THE MOON ᔓ Around the Moon by Jules Verne ᔓ THE WORLD ᔓ The Wonder
rroll, Great Expectations by Charles Dickens, Adventures of Huckleberry Finn by Mark Twain, A Christmas Carol by Charles Dickens, Moby-Dick by Herman Melville, The Secret Garden by Frances Hodgson Burnett, Heidi by
wiss Family Robinson by Johann David Wyss, Robinson Crusoe by Daniel Defoe, The Count of Monte Cristo by Alexandre Dumas, Kidnapped by Robert Louis Stevenson, Gulliver's Travels by Jonathan Swift and Twenty Thousa
nd Leagues Under the Sea by Jules Verne ᔓ THE HOLE ᔓ Alice's Adventures in Wonderland by Lewis Carroll ᔓ THE MOUNTAINS ᔓ Peter Pan and Wendy by J.M. Barrie ᔓ THE CAVE ᔓ Treasure Island by Robert Lou
Grimm, Tom Thumb as told by Richard Johnson, The Golden Bird as told by Jacob Grimm and Wilhelm Grimm, Snow-White and Rose-Red as told by Jacob Grimm and Wilhelm Grimm, Beauty and the Beast by Jeanne-Marie Lep
Grimm and Wilhelm Grimm ᔓ THE CLOUDS ᔓ Suo Gân as adapted by Robert Bryan, Twinkle, Twinkle, Little Star by Jane Taylor, Hush-a-Bye Baby as adapted by John Newbery and Brahms' Lullaby by Johannes Brahms ᔓ T
ale of Peter Rabbit by Beatrix Potter, Alice's Adventures in Wonderland by Lewis Carroll, Great Expectations by Charles Dickens, Adventures of Huckleberry Finn by Mark Twain, A Christmas Carol by Charles Dickens, Moby
ashington Irving ᔓ THE SEA ᔓ The Voyages of Doctor Dolittle by Hugh Lofting, The Swiss Family Robinson by Johann David Wyss, Robinson Crusoe by Daniel Defoe, The Count of Monte Cristo by Alexandre Dumas, Kidn
hann David Wyss, The Adventures of Pinocchio by Carlo Collodi and Twenty Thousand Leagues Under the Sea by Jules Verne ᔓ THE HOLE ᔓ Alice's Adventures in Wonderland by Lewis Carroll ᔓ THE MOUNTAINS ᔓ P
Grimm and Wilhelm Grimm, The Golden Goose as told by Jacob Grimm and Wilhelm Grimm, Tom Thumb as told by Richard Johnson, The Golden Bird as told by Jacob Grimm and Wilhelm Grimm, Snow-White and Rose-Red
by Mary Shelley and Dracula by Bram Stoker ᔓ THE ROPE ᔓ Rapunzel as told by Jacob Grimm and Wilhelm Grimm ᔓ THE CLOUDS ᔓ Suo Gân as adapted by Robert Bryan, Twinkle, Twinkle, Little Star by Jane Taylor, Hu
Grahame, Little Women by Louisa May Alcott, The Three Musketeers by Alexandre Dumas, The Tale of Peter Rabbit by Beatrix Potter, Alice's Adventures in Wonderland by Lewis Carroll, Great Expectations by Charles Dickens,
ur and His Knights by Sir Thomas Malory and Sir James Knowles and Rip Van Winkle by Washington Irving ᔓ THE SEA ᔓ The Voyages of Doctor Dolittle by Hugh Lofting, The Swiss Family Robinson by Johann David Wyss, F
s by Jonathan Swift, Robinson Crusoe by Daniel Defoe, The Swiss Family Robinson by Johann David Wyss, The Adventures of Pinocchio by Carlo Collodi and Twenty Thousand Leagues Under the Sea by Jules Verne ᔓ THE H
Red-Cap as told by Jacob Grimm and Wilhelm Grimm, Hansel & Gretel as told by Jacob Grimm and Wilhelm Grimm, The Golden Goose as told by Jacob Grimm and Wilhelm Grimm, Tom Thumb as told by Richard Johnson, The
HE MONSTER ᔓ The Legend of Sleepy Hollow by Washington Irving, Frankenstein by Mary Shelley and Dracula by Bram Stoker ᔓ THE ROPE ᔓ Rapunzel as told by Jacob Grimm and Wilhelm Grimm ᔓ THE CLOUDS
Wonderful Wizard of Oz by L. Frank Baum, The Wind in the Willows by Kenneth Grahame, Little Women by Louisa May Alcott, The Three Musketeers by Alexandre Dumas, The Tale of Peter Rabbit by Beatrix Potter, Alice's Ad
tt, Heidi by Johanna Spyri, Black Beauty by Anna Sewell, The Legends of King Arthur and His Knights by Sir Thomas Malory and Sir James Knowles and Rip Van Winkle by Washington Irving ᔓ THE SEA ᔓ The Voyages of D
Thousand Leagues Under the Sea by Jules Verne ᔓ THE WAVE ᔓ Gulliver's Travels by Jonathan Swift, Robinson Crusoe by Daniel Defoe, The Swiss Family Robinson by Johann David Wyss, The Adventures of Pinocchio by
ouis Stevenson and Kidnapped by Robert Louis Stevenson ᔓ THE FOREST ᔓ Little Red-Cap as told by Jacob Grimm and Wilhelm Grimm, Hansel & Gretel as told by Jacob Grimm and Wilhelm Grimm, The Golden Goose as tol
prince de Beaumont and Rapunzel as told by Jacob Grimm and Wilhelm Grimm ᔓ THE MONSTER ᔓ The Legend of Sleepy Hollow by Washington Irving, Frankenstein by Mary Shelley and Dracula by Bram Stoker ᔓ THE RO
THE MOON ᔓ Around the Moon by Jules Verne ᔓ THE WORLD ᔓ The Wonderful Wizard of Oz by L. Frank Baum, The Wind in the Willows by Kenneth Grahame, Little Women by Louisa May Alcott, The Three Musket
y-Dick by Herman Melville, The Secret Garden by Frances Hodgson Burnett, Heidi by Johanna Spyri, Black Beauty by Anna Sewell, The Legends of King Arthur and His Knights by Sir Thomas Malory and Sir James Knowles and
by Robert Louis Stevenson, Gulliver's Travels by Jonathan Swift and Twenty Thousand Leagues Under the Sea by Jules Verne ᔓ THE WAVE ᔓ Gulliver's Travels by Jonathan Swift, Robinson Crusoe by Daniel Defoe, The Swiss F
and Wendy by J.M. Barrie ᔓ THE CAVE ᔓ Treasure Island by Robert Louis Stevenson and Kidnapped by Robert Louis Stevenson ᔓ THE FOREST ᔓ Little Red-Cap as told by Jacob Grimm and Wilhelm Grimm, Hansel & Gre
b Grimm and Wilhelm Grimm, Beauty and the Beast by Jeanne-Marie Leprince de Beaumont and Rapunzel as told by Jacob Grimm and Wilhelm Grimm ᔓ THE MONSTER ᔓ The Legend of Sleepy Hollow by Washington Irving
s adapted by John Newbery and Brahms' Lullaby by Johannes Brahms ᔓ THE MOON ᔓ Around the Moon by Jules Verne ᔓ THE WORLD ᔓ The Wonderful Wizard of Oz by L. Frank Baum, The Wind in the Willows by Ken
eberry Finn by Mark Twain, A Christmas Carol by Charles Dickens, Moby-Dick by Herman Melville, The Secret Garden by Frances Hodgson Burnett, Heidi by Johanna Spyri, Black Beauty by Anna Sewell, The Legends of King
aniel Defoe, The Count of Monte Cristo by Alexandre Dumas, Kidnapped by Robert Louis Stevenson, Gulliver's Travels by Jonathan Swift and Twenty Thousand Leagues Under the Sea by Jules Verne ᔓ THE WAVE ᔓ Gulliver's
Adventures in Wonderland by Lewis Carroll ᔓ THE MOUNTAINS ᔓ Peter Pan and Wendy by J.M. Barrie ᔓ THE CAVE ᔓ Treasure Island by Robert Louis Stevenson and Kidnapped by Robert Louis Stevenson ᔓ THE FORES
as told by Jacob Grimm and Wilhelm Grimm, Snow-White and Rose-Red as told by Jacob Grimm and Wilhelm Grimm, Beauty and the Beast by Jeanne-Marie Leprince de Beaumont and Rapunzel as told by Jacob Grimm and Wilh
s adapted by Robert Bryan, Twinkle, Twinkle, Little Star by Jane Taylor, Hush-a-Bye Baby as adapted by John Newbery and Brahms' Lullaby by Johannes Brahms ᔓ THE MOON ᔓ Around the Moon by Jules Verne ᔓ THE WOR
n Wonderland by Lewis Carroll, Great Expectations by Charles Dickens, Adventures of Huckleberry Finn by Mark Twain, A Christmas Carol by Charles Dickens, Moby-Dick by Herman Melville, The Secret Garden by Frances
by Hugh Lofting, The Swiss Family Robinson by Johann David Wyss, Robinson Crusoe by Daniel Defoe, The Count of Monte Cristo by Alexandre Dumas, Kidnapped by Robert Louis Stevenson, Gulliver's Travels by Jonathan Sw
and Twenty Thousand Leagues Under the Sea by Jules Verne ᔓ THE HOLE ᔓ Alice's Adventures in Wonderland by Lewis Carroll ᔓ THE MOUNTAINS ᔓ Peter Pan and Wendy by J.M. Barrie ᔓ THE CAVE ᔓ Treasure I
rimm and Wilhelm Grimm, Tom Thumb as told by Richard Johnson, The Golden Bird as told by Jacob Grimm and Wilhelm Grimm, Snow-White and Rose-Red as told by Jacob Grimm and Wilhelm Grimm, Beauty and the Beast
punzel as told by Jacob Grimm and Wilhelm Grimm ᔓ THE CLOUDS ᔓ Suo Gân as adapted by Robert Bryan, Twinkle, Twinkle, Little Star by Jane Taylor, Hush-a-Bye Baby as adapted by John Newbery and Brahms' Lullaby by
exandre Dumas, The Tale of Peter Rabbit by Beatrix Potter, Alice's Adventures in Wonderland by Lewis Carroll, Great Expectations by Charles Dickens, Adventures of Huckleberry Finn by Mark Twain, A Christmas Carol by C
an Winkle by Washington Irving ᔓ THE SEA ᔓ The Voyages of Doctor Dolittle by Hugh Lofting, The Swiss Family Robinson by Johann David Wyss, Robinson Crusoe by Daniel Defoe, The Count of Monte Cristo by Alexand
Family Robinson by Johann David Wyss, The Adventures of Pinocchio by Carlo Collodi and Twenty Thousand Leagues Under the Sea by Jules Verne ᔓ THE HOLE ᔓ Alice's Adventures in Wonderland by Lewis Carroll ᔓ TH
etel as told by Jacob Grimm and Wilhelm Grimm, The Golden Goose as told by Jacob Grimm and Wilhelm Grimm, Tom Thumb as told by Richard Johnson, The Golden Bird as told by Jacob Grimm and Wilhelm Grimm, Snow-Whi
g, Frankenstein by Mary Shelley and Dracula by Bram Stoker ᔓ THE ROPE ᔓ Rapunzel as told by Jacob Grimm and Wilhelm Grimm ᔓ THE CLOUDS ᔓ Suo Gân as adapted by Robert Bryan, Twinkle, Twinkle, Little Star by
s by Kenneth Grahame, Little Women by Louisa May Alcott, The Three Musketeers by Alexandre Dumas, The Tale of Peter Rabbit by Beatrix Potter, Alice's Adventures in Wonderland by Lewis Carroll, Great Expectations by Ch
s of King Arthur and His Knights by Sir Thomas Malory and Sir James Knowles and Rip Van Winkle by Washington Irving ᔓ THE SEA ᔓ The Voyages of Doctor Dolittle by Hugh Lofting, The Swiss Family Robinson by Johan
Gulliver's Travels by Jonathan Swift, Robinson Crusoe by Daniel Defoe, The Swiss Family Robinson by Johann David Wyss, The Adventures of Pinocchio by Carlo Collodi and Twenty Thousand Leagues Under the Sea by Ju
FOREST ᔓ Little Red-Cap as told by Jacob Grimm and Wilhelm Grimm, Hansel & Gretel as told by Jacob Grimm and Wilhelm Grimm, The Golden Goose as told by Jacob Grimm and Wilhelm Grimm, Tom Thumb as told by Rich
lhelm Grimm ᔓ THE MONSTER ᔓ The Legend of Sleepy Hollow by Washington Irving, Frankenstein by Mary Shelley and Dracula by Bram Stoker ᔓ THE ROPE ᔓ Rapunzel as told by Jacob Grimm and Wilhelm Grimm ᔓ T
LD ᔓ The Wonderful Wizard of Oz by L. Frank Baum, The Wind in the Willows by Kenneth Grahame, Little Women by Louisa May Alcott, The Three Musketeers by Alexandre Dumas, The Tale of Peter Rabbit by Beatrix Pott
s Hodgson Burnett, Heidi by Johanna Spyri, Black Beauty by Anna Sewell, The Legends of King Arthur and His Knights by Sir Thomas Malory and Sir James Knowles and Rip Van Winkle by Washington Irving ᔓ THE SEA ᔓ Th
an Swift and Twenty Thousand Leagues Under the Sea by Jules Verne ᔓ THE WAVE ᔓ Gulliver's Travels by Jonathan Swift, Robinson Crusoe by Daniel Defoe, The Swiss Family Robinson by Johann David Wyss, The Adventu
ure Island by Robert Louis Stevenson and Kidnapped by Robert Louis Stevenson ᔓ THE FOREST ᔓ Little Red-Cap as told by Jacob Grimm and Wilhelm Grimm, Hansel & Gretel as told by Jacob Grimm and Wilhelm Grimm, The
ast by Jeanne-Marie Leprince de Beaumont and Rapunzel as told by Jacob Grimm and Wilhelm Grimm ᔓ THE MONSTER ᔓ The Legend of Sleepy Hollow by Washington Irving, Frankenstein by Mary Shelley and Dracula by Bra
by Johannes Brahms ᔓ THE MOON ᔓ Around the Moon by Jules Verne ᔓ THE WORLD ᔓ The Wonderful Wizard of Oz by L. Frank Baum, The Wind in the Willows by Kenneth Grahame, Little Women by Louisa May Alcot
ol by Charles Dickens, Moby-Dick by Herman Melville, The Secret Garden by Frances Hodgson Burnett, Heidi by Johanna Spyri, Black Beauty by Anna Sewell, The Legends of King Arthur and His Knights by Sir Thomas Malory
Alexandre Dumas, Kidnapped by Robert Louis Stevenson, Gulliver's Travels by Jonathan Swift and Twenty Thousand Leagues Under the Sea by Jules Verne ᔓ THE WAVE ᔓ Gulliver's Travels by Jonathan Swift, Robinson Cruso
E MOUNTAINS ᔓ Peter Pan and Wendy by J.M. Barrie ᔓ THE CAVE ᔓ Treasure Island by Robert Louis Stevenson and Kidnapped by Robert Louis Stevenson ᔓ THE FOREST ᔓ Little Red-Cap as told by Jacob Grimm and W

Extract from "The Speed of Darkness" from Muriel Rukeyser's *The Speed of Darkness,* New York:
Random House, 1968, included here with kind permission of ICM Partners, New York

All reasonable efforts have been made to trace the copyright holders and secure permission for the use of material used herein.
The publisher will be happy to make any necessary corrections in future printings.

First U.S. edition 2016

Library of Congress Catalog Card Number 2016943940
ISBN 978-0-7636-9077-9

16 17 18 19 20 21 CCP 10 9 8 7 6 5 4 3 2

Printed in Shenzhen, Guangdong, China

This book was hand-lettered,
and the typographical landscapes
were typeset in Adobe Garamond Pro.
The illustrations were done in watercolor,
pencil, and digital collage.

Candlewick Press
99 Dover Street
Somerville, Massachusetts 02144

visit us at www.candlewick.com

CANDLEWICK PRESS

A Child of Books

oliver JEFFERS
SAM winston

I am a
child of Books.

I come from
a WORLD of STORIES

Once upon a time
there was a child who
loved to read

and upon my
IMAGINation

I Float.

...a vain refuge, that trembled and shook before the to... the atmosphere with its mighty wings; from time to t... across the heavens like a fiery serpent, lighting up the clouds tha... of the keeper. The latter, sure of quelling the tempest when the waves became too viole... them to rise to a certain pitch that he might be revenged on the importunate An... besides it would afford him some recreation during the day. **Kidnapped** While I... the brig, I spied a tract of water lying between us where no great waves came, b... yet boiled white all over and bristled in the moon with rings and bubbles. Some... whole tract swung to one side, like the tail of a live serpent; sometimes, for a gl... it would all disappear and then boil up again. What it was I had no guess, which... time increased my fear of it; but I now know it must have been the roost or tid... which had carried me away so fast and tumbled me about so cruelly, and at last... of that play, had flung out me and the spare yard upon its landward margin... **Gulliver's Travels** It would not be proper, for some reasons, to trouble the re... culars of our adventures in those seas; let it suffice to inform him, that in our p... ence to the East Indies, we were driven by a violent storm to the north-west... Diemen's Land. By an observation, we found ourselves in the latitude of 30 d... 2 minutes south. Twelve of our crew were dead by immoderate labour and il... the rest were in a very weak condition. On the 5th of November, which was th... of summer in those parts, the weather being very hazy, the seamen spied... within half a cable's length of the ship; but the wind was so strong, that we we... directly upon it, and immediately split. Six of the crew, of whom I was one... let down the boat into the sea, made a shift to get clear of the ship and the r... We rowed, by my computation, about three leagues, till we were able to work n... being already spent with labour while we were in the ship. We therefore tru... ourselves to the mercy of the waves, and in about half an hour the boat was over... a sudden flurry from the north. What became of my companions in the boat, a... as of those who escaped on the rock, or were left in the vessel, I cannot tell; but c... they were all lost. For my own part, I swam as fortune directed me, and was pe... forward by wind and tide. I often let my legs drop, and could feel no bottom; but... I was almost gone, and able to struggle no longer, I found myself within my de... near a mile before I got to the shore, which I conjectured was about eight o'c... the evening. I then advanced forward near half a mile, but could not disc... sign of houses or inhabitants; at least I was in so weak a condition, that... observe them. I was extremely tired, and with that, and the heat of... ther, and about half a pint of brandy that I drank as I left the ship, I... myself much inclined to sleep. I lay down on the grass, which was v... hort and soft, where I slept sounder than ever I remember to have d... my life, and, as I reckoned, about nine hours; for when I awaked, it... just day-light. I attempted to rise, but was not able to stir: for, as I... to lie on my back, I found my arms and legs were strongly fa... on each side to the ground; and my hair, which was long and th... down in the same manner. I likewise felt several slender liga... across my body, from my arm-pits to my thighs. I could only lo... wards; the sun began to grow hot, and the light offended my e... heard a confused noise about me; but in the posture I lay, co... nothing except the sky. In a little time I felt something alive... on my left leg, which advancing gently forward over my br... came almost up to my chin; when, bending my eyes down w... much as I could, I perceived it to be a human creature no... inches high, with a bow and arrow in his hands, and a quive... back. In the mean time, I felt at least forty more. I was of t... However, they soon returned, and one of them, who ven... so far as to get a full sight of my face, lifting up his hands a... by way of admiration, cried out in a shrill but distinct voic... the others repeated the same words several times, n... I knew not what they meant. I lay all this while, as the re... may believe, in great uneasiness. **Twenty Thousand Leagues**... **Under the Sea** So our salvation lay totally in the hands of th... mysterious helmsmen steering this submersible, and if it made a...

I have SAILED
ACROSS a SEA
of WORDS

To ask if you will
COME AWAY with ME.

SOME PEOPLE have
FORGOTTEN where
I live

BUSINESS

large business has rejected a
takeover proposal from another
large business which valued the first
large business for "a lot of money."
The large business said it offered "a
lot of money" and then "even more
money" but the first large business
said "that wasn't enough money"
and it wouldn't be bought out. The
first large business issued a warning
in January saying it hadn't made "a
lot of money" which prompted the
second large business to think about
buying it. "The question is, does the
large business have the money
first business?" an industry
commented.

other businesses got excited
this idea and started talking about
how much money each business was
worth. This made everyone worried
and excited, and they all waved their
arms around and jumped

IMPORTANT THINGS

portant company is to stop
ing some important stuff by
is year. It said no one wanted
rticular bit of important stuff.
ne from a website said – "It's
all surprising that they have
d producing this thing –
s it's not so important after all
main issue now is to find other
that might be important."

company announced it would
d focus on producing other bits
ff that they hoped the public
s find important. "We remain
gitted to providing people with
tant things and if we can't do
hen we will pretend they are
tant and hopefully that will
aid the leading inventor at the
any.

also said they would stop making this
particular bit of stuff as they also thought
it might not be as important as they once
thought it was. "What makes something
really important nowadays is how much
money we spend on it and if we spend
vast amounts of money on it, then that
obviously means it's going to be really
important and we will certainly make a
hoo-haa about it when we put it in the
shops," said the Big Boss.

One customer did respond to this
comment with "My cat is very important
and that didn't cost anything!" to which
the important company wrote a letter
in response that said, "Dear Customer,
we understand that you think your cat
is very important but unfortunately you
are wrong in this matter. Our leading
inventor says he didn't invent your

Serious Stuff

A group of serious people passed on concerns about a serious document that has been lost by a serious
organization. The serious people asked officials a long time ago to "look carefully" at this
document – the serious organization initially said it had looked at this serious document last y
concluded that "it wasn't that serious" and then went on to say "we have lost it." Someone els
looked at this document said "actually it was serious and I hope they find it." In an earlier ver
story, we reported that the serious
organization had started looking
for the serious document. In fact,
they started looking last year.
So far they have looked "under
chairs, rugs, and even down a
sofa." Someone suggested to try
looking "on the computer" but
that was unsuccessful as it wasn't
turned on.

In other cases like this – when
someone says "this is serious" and
the other says "no it isn't" – they
often have to find a third person
to tell them whether it's serious
or not. One of the problems with

THE FACTS

Scientists have discovered a
new fact. In one test, nearly
half the subjects proved the
fact, it was revealed. The
findings, which came from
first watching people and
then quizzing them, have
attracted criticism from some
other scientists.

The paper, published in a
magazine about facts, said
that their fact was true.
A professor, who led the
research at a university, said:
"Our study demonstrated
____" This might

kind of thing but for o
who don't – it could be rather
alarming.

In fact, other researchers in
the field have said the findings
are overstated. The authors
say this 'fact' might have
been overlooked in research.
Their work began with several
trials involving people who
were shut in a small room
and tested. After 6, 12, or 15
minutes, they were asked if
they had discovered this fact.
On average, their answers
were near the middle of a
nine-point scale.

"It
is
a long
tail, certainly,"
said Alice,
looking down
with wonder at
the Mouse's tail;
"but why do you
call it sad?" And
she kept puzzling
about it while the
Mouse was speaking,
so that her idea of the
tale was something like
this: "Fury said to a mouse,
That he met in the house, 'Let
us both go to law: I will prosecute
YOU.—Come, I'll take no
denial; We must have a trial:
For really this morning I've
nothing to do.' Said the mouse
to the cur, 'Such a trial, dear sir,
With no jury or judge, would
be wasting our breath.' 'I'll be
judge, I'll be jury,' said cunning
old Fury: 'I'll try the whole cause, and
condemn you to death.' *Alice's Adventures
in Wonderland* The rabbit-hole went stra
then dipped suddenly down, so sud   that Alice had not a
moment to think about sto   lf before she found herself falling down what seemed to be a very deep well.
Either the well was very deep, or she fell very slowly, for she had plenty of time as she went down to look about her, and to
nothing of tumbling down stairs! How brave they'll all think me at home! W
Down, down, down. Would the fall never come to an
getting somewhere near the centre
Presently she began a

But along these WORDS
I can show you the WAY.

wonder what was going to happen next. First, she tried to look down and make out what but it was too dark t

y, I wouldn't say anything about it, even if I fell off the top of the was very likely true.

end? "I wonder how many miles I've fallen by this time aloud. "I must

of the earth. Let me see: that would be four thousand miles down, I

gain. "I wonder if I shall fall right through the earth How funny

Down, down, down. There was nothing else to do so Alice soon

WE will TRAVEL over

MOUNTAINS of MAKE-BEliEVE

the story had been told for the night, and Jane was now asleep in her bed. Wendy was sitting on the floor, very close to the fire,

r f a
i l
l
h i

light in the nursery; and while she sat darning she heard a crow. Then the window blew open as of old, and Peter dropped on the floor. He was exactly the same as ever, and Wendy saw at once that he still had all his first teeth. He was a little boy, and she was grown up. She huddled by the fire not daring to move, helpless and guilty, a big woman. "Hullo, Wendy," he said, not noticing any difference, for he was thinking chiefly of himself; and in the dim light her white dress might have been the nightgown in which he had seen her first. "Hullo, Peter," she replied faintly, squeezing herself as small

"Hullo,
"Yes."
"Boy or girl?"
Now
Girl."

he would

Her w

Peter Pan and Wendy

gs would scarcely carry her now. *Peter Pan and Wendy* on his shoulder and gave his nose a loving bite. She whispered in his ear "You silly ass," and then, tottering to her chamber, lay down on the bed. His head almost filled the fourth wall of her little room as he knelt near her in distress. There were no children there, and it was night-time; but he addressed all who might be dreaming of the Neverland, and who were therefore believed in fairies. Peter flung out his arms. There were no children there, and it was night-that she thought she could get well again if children believed in fairies. Peter flung out his arms. There were no children there, and it was night-beautiful finger and let them run over it. Her voice was so low that at first he could not make out what she said. Then he made it out. She was saying that she put out her hand and let them run over it. Her voice was growing fainter; but he knew that if it went out she would be no more. She liked his tears so much that he put out her arms. There were no children there, and it was night-boys and girls in their nighties. "Do you believe?" he cried. Tink sat up in bed almost brisky to listen to her fate. She fancied she heard answers in the affirmative, and then again she shouted to them, "clap your hands; don't let Tink die." Many clapped. Some didn't. A few wasn't sure. "What do you think?" she asked Peter. "If you believe," he earth was happening; but already Tink flashing through the room more merry and impudent than ever. She never believed, but she would have liked to get at the ones who had hissed. "And now to rescue Wendy!"

It have not chosen such had hoped to fly

beasts hissed. The clapping stopped suddenly; as if countless mothers had rushed to their nurseries to see what on earth was happening; but she popped out of bed, then she was flashing through the room more merry and impudent than ever. She never thought of thanking those who believed, but she would have liked to get at the ones who had hissed. "And now to rescue Wendy!"

The moon was riding in his cloudy heaven when Peter rose from his tree, wearing on his little stupid perilous self, with weapons an else,

now; and she ran out of the room to try to think. Peter continued to cry, and soon his sobs woke Jane. She sat up in bed, and was interested at once. "Boy," she said, "why are you crying?" Peter rose and bowed to her, and she bowed to him from the bed. "Hullo," he said. "Hullo," said Jane. "My name is Peter Pan," he explained. "Yes, I know." "I came back for my mother," he told her. "to take her to the Neverland." "Yes, I know," Jane said, "I have been waiting."

the sheet sitting on the bed,

DISCOVER TREASURE in the DARKNESS.

SQUIRE TRELAWNEY, Dr. Livesey, and the rest of these gentlemen having asked me to write down the whole particulars about Treasure Island, from the beginning to the end, keeping nothing back but the bearings of the island, and that only because there is still treasure not yet lifted, I take up my pen in the year of grace 17—and go back to the time when my father kept the Admiral Ben-bow inn and the brown old seaman with the sabre cut first took up his lodging under our roof.

"Fifteen men on the Dead man's Chest. Yo-ho-ho, and a bottle of rum!

Drink and the devil had done for the rest."

Treasure Island. The paper had been sealed in several places with a thimble by way of seal; the very thimble, perhaps, that I had found in the captain's pocket. The doctor opened the seals with great care, and there fell out the map of an island, with latitude and longitude, soundings, names of hills and bays and inlets, and every particular that would be needed to bring a ship to a safe anchorage upon its shores. It was about nine miles long and five across, shaped, you might say, like a fat dragon standing up, and had two fine land-locked harbours, and

"Bulk of treasure here." Over on the back the same hand had written this further informa
Tall tree, Spy- glass shoulder,
bearing a point to the N.
of N.E. Skeleton
Island E.S.E. and
by Ten feet.
silver!

With my arms before me I walked steadily in.

"Cap'n Silver, sir, Long John answered for himself. "By this time, I had got to my word, Cap'n," said Silver's green parrot out of the darkness; and

"Hang the treasure! It's the glory of the sea that has turned my head."

"If it comes to a swinging, swing all say I."

"Dead men don't bite"

of
sea-
dreams "and
the most
charming
anticipations of
strange islands and
adventures. I brooded by
the hour together over the
map, all the details of which I
remembered by the first

Little Red-Cap It was a ... "What will become of us; how can we feed our children, now that ... dancing to and fro through ... beautiful flowers ... Little Red-Cap was takin ... happy Little Red-Cap was

Hansel & Gretel Once upon a time there dwelt near a large wood ... a little boy called Hansel and ... named Gretel ... a girl ... woodcutter, two children, with his wife and ... in hollow under the roots a goose ... plumage of pure gold

The Golden Goose Dummerly set to work, and cut down ... when it fell ... tree ... "Oh, Father ... shall be in the wood ... cried ... into ...

One day, *Tom Thumb* ...

Then the fox said, "Do not shoot you good counsel: the golden bird. want to bird.

The Golden Bird

They saw a beautiful child in passed from sight. She arose white. into the wood, eyes opened their a snow-white

Snow-White & Rose-Red I all but said no word Once, when they had spent the night in the wood and the bright sunrise awoke them the wood in the wood

Beauty & The Beast thus standing large forest she was

Rapunzel, Rapunzel tree Let down your hair

WE can lose
ourselves in FORESTS
of FAIRY Tales

and ESCAPE MONStets in HAUNTED CASTLes.

she had magnificent long hair, fine as spun gold, and when she heard the voice of the prince, she unfastened her braided tresses, wound them round one of the hooks of the window above, and then the hair fell down

we will sleep

in clouds

of

SONG

and SHOUT as LOUD as we like in SPACE.

OUR HOUSE is a Home of

INVENTIon

I am a child of books. I come from a world of stories

made   from   house

stories   our   is   a

our   world   we've

where ANYONE at ALL can come

home   of   invention   where   anyone   at   all

con

can

all

For
IMAGINATION
is FREE

THE GOLDEN GOOSE *as told by Jacob Grimm and Wilhelm Grimm*, **Tom Thumb** *as told by Richard Johnson*, **The Golden Bird** *as told by Jacob Grimm and Wilhelm Grimm*, **The W** *and* **Red R** *by Jacob Grimm and W*
by Bram Stoker ✧ THE ROPE ✧ **Rapunzel** *as told by Jacob Grimm and Wilhelm Grimm* ✧ THE CLOUDS ✧ **Suo Gân** *as adapted by Robert Bryan*, **Twinkle, Twinkle, Little Star** *by Jane Taylor*, **Hush-a-Bye Baby** *as adapted by Jo*
ay Alcott, **The Three Musketeers** *by Alexandre Dumas*, **The Tale of Peter Rabbit** *by Beatrix Potter*, **Alice's Adventures in Wonderland** *by Lewis Carroll*, **Great Expectations** *by Charles Dickens*, **Adventures of Huckleberry Finn** *by*
Malory and Sir James Knowles and **Rip Van Winkle** *by Washington Irving* ✧ THE SEA ✧ **The Voyages of Doctor Dolittle** *by Hugh Lofting*, **The Swiss Family Robinson** *by Johann David Wyss*, **Robinson Crusoe** *by Daniel Defoe*,
n Crusoe by Daniel Defoe, **The Swiss Family Robinson** *by Johann David Wyss*, **The Adventures of Pinocchio** *by Carlo Collodi* and **Twenty Thousand Leagues Under the Sea** *by Jules Verne* ✧ THE HOLE ✧ **Alice's Adventures**
mm and Wilhelm Grimm, **Hansel & Gretel** *as told by Jacob Grimm and Wilhelm Grimm*, **The Golden Goose** *as told by Jacob Grimm and Wilhelm Grimm*, **Tom Thumb** *as told by Richard Johnson*, **The Golden Bird** *as told by Jacob*
and Sleepy Hollow by Washington Irving, **Frankenstein** *by Mary Shelley* and **Dracula** *by Bram Stoker* ✧ THE ROPE ✧ **Rapunzel** *as told by Jacob Grimm and Wilhelm Grimm* ✧ THE CLOUDS ✧ **Suo Gân** *as adapted by Rober*
k Baum, **The Wind in the Willows** *by Kenneth Grahame*, **Little Women** *by Louisa May Alcott*, **The Three Musketeers** *by Alexandre Dumas*, **The Tale of Peter Rabbit** *by Beatrix Potter*, **Alice's Adventures in Wonderland** *by Lewi*
auty by Anna Sewell, **The Legends of King Arthur and His Knights** *by Sir Thomas Malory and Sir James Knowles* and **Rip Van Winkle** *by Washington Irving* ✧ THE SEA ✧ **The Voyages of Doctor Dolittle** *by Hugh Lofting*,
he Sea by Jules Verne ✧ THE WAVE ✧ **Gulliver's Travels** *by Jonathan Swift*, **Robinson Crusoe** *by Daniel Defoe*, **The Swiss Family Robinson** *by Johann David Wyss*, **The Adventures of Pinocchio** *by Carlo Collodi* and **Twenty Tho**
ed by Robert Louis Stevenson ✧ THE FOREST ✧ **Little Red-Cap** *as told by Jacob Grimm and Wilhelm Grimm*, **Hansel & Gretel** *as told by Jacob Grimm and Wilhelm Grimm*, **The Golden Goose** *as told by Jacob Grimm and Wilhel*
unzel as told by Jacob Grimm and Wilhelm Grimm ✧ THE MONSTER ✧ **The Legend of Sleepy Hollow** *by Washington Irving*, **Frankenstein** *by Mary Shelley* and **Dracula** *by Bram Stoker* ✧ THE ROPE ✧ **Rapunzel** *as told by Ja*
the Moon by Jules Verne ✧ THE WORLD ✧ **The Wonderful Wizard of Oz** *by L. Frank Baum*, **The Wind in the Willows** *by Kenneth Grahame*, **Little Women** *by Louisa May Alcott*, **The Three Musketeers** *by Alexandre Dumas*, T
Melville, **The Secret Garden** *by Frances Hodgson Burnett*, **Heidi** *by Johanna Spyri*, **Black Beauty** *by Anna Sewell*, **The Legends of King Arthur and His Knights** *by Sir Thomas Malory and Sir James Knowles* and **Rip Van Winkle**
venson, **Gulliver's Travels** *by Jonathan Swift* and **Twenty Thousand Leagues Under the Sea** *by Jules Verne* ✧ THE WAVE ✧ **Gulliver's Travels** *by Jonathan Swift*, **Robinson Crusoe** *by Daniel Defoe*, **The Swiss Family Robinson** *b*
y J.M. Barrie ✧ THE CAVE ✧ **Treasure Island** *by Robert Louis Stevenson* and **Kidnapped** *by Robert Louis Stevenson* ✧ THE FOREST ✧ **Little Red-Cap** *as told by Jacob Grimm and Wilhelm Grimm*, **Hansel & Gretel** *as told by Ja*
nd Wilhelm Grimm, **Beauty and the Beast** *by Jeanne-Marie Leprince de Beaumont* and **Rapunzel** *as told by Jacob Grimm and Wilhelm Grimm* ✧ THE MONSTER ✧ **The Legend of Sleepy Hollow** *by Washington Irving*, Frankens
y John Newbery and **Brahms' Lullaby** *by Johannes Brahms* ✧ THE MOON ✧ **Around the Moon** *by Jules Verne* ✧ THE WORLD ✧ **The Wonderful Wizard of Oz** *by L. Frank Baum*, **The Wind in the Willows** *by Kenneth Graha*
n by Mark Twain, **A Christmas Carol** *by Charles Dickens*, **Moby-Dick** *by Herman Melville*, **The Secret Garden** *by Frances Hodgson Burnett*, **Heidi** *by Johanna Spyri*, **Black Beauty** *by Anna Sewell*, **The Legends of King Arthur an*
efoe, **The Count of Monte Cristo** *by Alexandre Dumas*, **Kidnapped** *by Robert Louis Stevenson*, **Gulliver's Travels** *by Jonathan Swift* and **Twenty Thousand Leagues Under the Sea** *by Jules Verne* ✧ THE WAVE ✧ **Gulliver's Travel**
res in Wonderland by Lewis Carroll ✧ THE MOUNTAINS ✧ **Peter Pan and Wendy** *by J.M. Barrie* ✧ THE CAVE ✧ **Treasure Island** *by Robert Louis Stevenson* and **Kidnapped** *by Robert Louis Stevenson* ✧ THE FOREST ✧ **Li**
cob Grimm and Wilhelm Grimm, **Snow-White and Rose-Red** *as told by Jacob Grimm and Wilhelm Grimm*, **Beauty and the Beast** *by Jeanne-Marie Leprince de Beaumont* and **Rapunzel** *as told by Jacob Grimm and Wilhelm Grimm*
y Robert Bryan, **Twinkle, Twinkle, Little Star** *by Jane Taylor*, **Hush-a-Bye Baby** *as adapted by John Newbery* and **Brahms' Lullaby** *by Johannes Brahms* ✧ THE MOON ✧ **Around the Moon** *by Jules Verne* ✧ THE WORLD ✧ Th
and by Lewis Carroll, **Great Expectations** *by Charles Dickens*, **Adventures of Huckleberry Finn** *by Mark Twain*, **A Christmas Carol** *by Charles Dickens*, **Moby-Dick** *by Herman Melville*, **The Secret Garden** *by Frances Hodgson Bu*
ting, **The Swiss Family Robinson** *by Johann David Wyss*, **Robinson Crusoe** *by Daniel Defoe*, **The Count of Monte Cristo** *by Alexandre Dumas*, **Kidnapped** *by Robert Louis Stevenson*, **Gulliver's Travels** *by Jonathan Swift* and **Twe**
Thousand Leagues Under the Sea by Jules Verne ✧ THE HOLE ✧ **Alice's Adventures in Wonderland** *by Lewis Carroll* ✧ THE MOUNTAINS ✧ **Peter Pan and Wendy** *by J.M. Barrie* ✧ THE CAVE ✧ **Treasure Island** *by Robe*
elm Grimm, **Tom Thumb** *as told by Richard Johnson*, **The Golden Bird** *as told by Jacob Grimm and Wilhelm Grimm*, **Snow-White and Rose-Red** *as told by Jacob Grimm and Wilhelm Grimm*, **Beauty and the Beast** *by Jeanne-Marie*
Jacob Grimm and Wilhelm Grimm ✧ THE CLOUDS ✧ **Suo Gân** *as adapted by Robert Bryan*, **Twinkle, Twinkle, Little Star** *by Jane Taylor*, **Hush-a-Bye Baby** *as adapted by John Newbery* and **Brahms' Lullaby** *by Johannes Brahms*
The Tale of Peter Rabbit *by Beatrix Potter*, **Alice's Adventures in Wonderland** *by Lewis Carroll*, **Great Expectations** *by Charles Dickens*, **Adventures of Huckleberry Finn** *by Mark Twain*, **A Christmas Carol** *by Charles Dickens*, M
gton Irving ✧ THE SEA ✧ **The Voyages of Doctor Dolittle** *by Hugh Lofting*, **The Swiss Family Robinson** *by Johann David Wyss*, **Robinson Crusoe** *by Daniel Defoe*, **The Count of Monte Cristo** *by Alexandre Dumas*, **Kidnapp**
David Wyss, **The Adventures of Pinocchio** *by Carlo Collodi* and **Twenty Thousand Leagues Under the Sea** *by Jules Verne* ✧ THE HOLE ✧ **Alice's Adventures in Wonderland** *by Lewis Carroll* ✧ THE MOUNTAINS ✧ Peter
nd Wilhelm Grimm, **The Golden Goose** *as told by Jacob Grimm and Wilhelm Grimm*, **Tom Thumb** *as told by Richard Johnson*, **The Golden Bird** *as told by Jacob Grimm and Wilhelm Grimm*, **Snow-White and Rose-Red** *as told by J*
lley and **Dracula** *by Bram Stoker* ✧ THE ROPE ✧ **Rapunzel** *as told by Jacob Grimm and Wilhelm Grimm* ✧ THE CLOUDS ✧ **Suo Gân** *as adapted by Robert Bryan*, **Twinkle, Twinkle, Little Star** *by Jane Taylor*, **Hush-a-Bye Bab**
omen by Louisa May Alcott, **The Three Musketeers** *by Alexandre Dumas*, **The Tale of Peter Rabbit** *by Beatrix Potter*, **Alice's Adventures in Wonderland** *by Lewis Carroll*, **Great Expectations** *by Charles Dickens*, **Adventures of Hu**
by Sir Thomas Malory and Sir James Knowles and **Rip Van Winkle** *by Washington Irving* ✧ THE SEA ✧ **The Voyages of Doctor Dolittle** *by Hugh Lofting*, **The Swiss Family Robinson** *by Johann David Wyss*, **Robinson Crusoe** *by*
Swift, **Robinson Crusoe** *by Daniel Defoe*, **The Swiss Family Robinson** *by Johann David Wyss*, **The Adventures of Pinocchio** *by Carlo Collodi* and **Twenty Thousand Leagues Under the Sea** *by Jules Verne* ✧ THE HOLE ✧ Alice
as told by Jacob Grimm and Wilhelm Grimm, **Hansel & Gretel** *as told by Jacob Grimm and Wilhelm Grimm*, **The Golden Goose** *as told by Jacob Grimm and Wilhelm Grimm*, **Tom Thumb** *as told by Richard Johnson*, **The Golden B**
NSTER ✧ **The Legend of Sleepy Hollow** *by Washington Irving*, **Frankenstein** *by Mary Shelley* and **Dracula** *by Bram Stoker* ✧ THE ROPE ✧ **Rapunzel** *as told by Jacob Grimm and Wilhelm Grimm* ✧ THE CLOUDS ✧ Suo
ul Wizard of Oz by L. Frank Baum, **The Wind in the Willows** *by Kenneth Grahame*, **Little Women** *by Louisa May Alcott*, **The Three Musketeers** *by Alexandre Dumas*, **The Tale of Peter Rabbit** *by Beatrix Potter*, **Alice's Adventure**
Johanna Spyri, **Black Beauty** *by Anna Sewell*, **The Legends of King Arthur and His Knights** *by Sir Thomas Malory and Sir James Knowles* and **Rip Van Winkle** *by Washington Irving* ✧ THE SEA ✧ **The Voyages of Doctor Dolit**
d Leagues Under the Sea by Jules Verne ✧ THE WAVE ✧ **Gulliver's Travels** *by Jonathan Swift*, **Robinson Crusoe** *by Daniel Defoe*, **The Swiss Family Robinson** *by Johann David Wyss*, **The Adventures of Pinocchio** *by Carlo Coll*
*venson and **Kidnapped** *by Robert Louis Stevenson* ✧ THE FOREST ✧ **Little Red-Cap** *as told by Jacob Grimm and Wilhelm Grimm*, **Hansel & Gretel** *as told by Jacob Grimm and Wilhelm Grimm*, **The Golden Goose** *as told by Jacob*
de Beaumont and **Rapunzel** *as told by Jacob Grimm and Wilhelm Grimm* ✧ THE MONSTER ✧ **The Legend of Sleepy Hollow** *by Washington Irving*, **Frankenstein** *by Mary Shelley* and **Dracula** *by Bram Stoker* ✧ THE ROPE ✧*
MOON ✧ **Around the Moon** *by Jules Verne* ✧ THE WORLD ✧ **The Wonderful Wizard of Oz** *by L. Frank Baum*, **The Wind in the Willows** *by Kenneth Grahame*, **Little Women** *by Louisa May Alcott*, **The Three Musketeers**
ick by Herman Melville, **The Secret Garden** *by Frances Hodgson Burnett*, **Heidi** *by Johanna Spyri*, **Black Beauty** *by Anna Sewell*, **The Legends of King Arthur and His Knights** *by Sir Thomas Malory and Sir James Knowles* and **Rip**
ed by Robert Louis Stevenson, **Gulliver's Travels** *by Jonathan Swift* and **Twenty Thousand Leagues Under the Sea** *by Jules Verne* ✧ THE WAVE ✧ **Gulliver's Travels** *by Jonathan Swift*, **Robinson Crusoe** *by Daniel Defoe*, **The Swi**
Pan and Wendy *by J.M. Barrie* ✧ THE CAVE ✧ **Treasure Island** *by Robert Louis Stevenson* and **Kidnapped** *by Robert Louis Stevenson* ✧ THE FOREST ✧ **Little Red-Cap** *as told by Jacob Grimm and Wilhelm Grimm*, **Hansel &**
Jacob Grimm and Wilhelm Grimm, **Beauty and the Beast** *by Jeanne-Marie Leprince de Beaumont* and **Rapunzel** *as told by Jacob Grimm and Wilhelm Grimm* ✧ THE MONSTER ✧ **The Legend of Sleepy Hollow** *by Washington Ir*
Bye Baby *as adapted by John Newbery* and **Brahms' Lullaby** *by Johannes Brahms* ✧ THE MOON ✧ **Around the Moon** *by Jules Verne* ✧ THE WORLD ✧ **The Wonderful Wizard of Oz** *by L. Frank Baum*, **The Wind in the Wille**
res of Huckleberry Finn by Mark Twain, **A Christmas Carol** *by Charles Dickens*, **Moby-Dick** *by Herman Melville*, **The Secret Garden** *by Frances Hodgson Burnett*, **Heidi** *by Johanna Spyri*, **Black Beauty** *by Anna Sewell*, **The Leger**
n Crusoe by Daniel Defoe, **The Count of Monte Cristo** *by Alexandre Dumas*, **Kidnapped** *by Robert Louis Stevenson*, **Gulliver's Travels** *by Jonathan Swift* and **Twenty Thousand Leagues Under the Sea** *by Jules Verne* ✧ THE WAV*
Alice's Adventures in Wonderland *by Lewis Carroll* ✧ THE MOUNTAINS ✧ **Peter Pan and Wendy** *by J.M. Barrie* ✧ THE CAVE ✧ **Treasure Island** *by Robert Louis Stevenson* and **Kidnapped** *by Robert Louis Stevenson* ✧ TH*
Bird *as told by Jacob Grimm and Wilhelm Grimm*, **Snow-White and Rose-Red** *as told by Jacob Grimm and Wilhelm Grimm*, **Beauty and the Beast** *by Jeanne-Marie Leprince de Beaumont* and **Rapunzel** *as told by Jacob Grimm and W*
as adapted by Robert Bryan, **Twinkle, Twinkle, Little Star** *by Jane Taylor*, **Hush-a-Bye Baby** *as adapted by John Newbery* and **Brahms' Lullaby** *by Johannes Brahms* ✧ THE MOON ✧ **Around the Moon** *by Jules Verne* ✧ THE WC*
res in Wonderland by Lewis Carroll, **Great Expectations** *by Charles Dickens*, **Adventures of Huckleberry Finn** *by Mark Twain*, **A Christmas Carol** *by Charles Dickens*, **Moby-Dick** *by Herman Melville*, **The Secret Garden** *by Fran*
Dolittle *by Hugh Lofting*, **The Swiss Family Robinson** *by Johann David Wyss*, **Robinson Crusoe** *by Daniel Defoe*, **The Count of Monte Cristo** *by Alexandre Dumas*, **Kidnapped** *by Robert Louis Stevenson*, **Gulliver's Travels** *by Jona*
Collodi and **Twenty Thousand Leagues Under the Sea** *by Jules Verne* ✧ THE HOLE ✧ **Alice's Adventures in Wonderland** *by Lewis Carroll* ✧ THE MOUNTAINS ✧ **Peter Pan and Wendy** *by J.M. Barrie* ✧ THE CAVE ✧ Tre*
cob Grimm and Wilhelm Grimm, **Tom Thumb** *as told by Richard Johnson*, **The Golden Bird** *as told by Jacob Grimm and Wilhelm Grimm*, **Snow-White and Rose-Red** *as told by Jacob Grimm and Wilhelm Grimm*, **Beauty and the**
Rapunzel *as told by Jacob Grimm and Wilhelm Grimm* ✧ THE CLOUDS ✧ **Suo Gân** *as adapted by Robert Bryan*, **Twinkle, Twinkle, Little Star** *by Jane Taylor*, **Hush-a-Bye Baby** *as adapted by John Newbery* and **Brahms'**
rs by Alexandre Dumas, **The Tale of Peter Rabbit** *by Beatrix Potter*, **Alice's Adventures in Wonderland** *by Lewis Carroll*, **Great Expectations** *by Charles Dickens*, **Adventures of Huckleberry Finn** *by Mark Twain*, **A Christmas C**
Rip Van Winkle *by Washington Irving* ✧ THE SEA ✧ **The Voyages of Doctor Dolittle** *by Hugh Lofting*, **The Swiss Family Robinson** *by Johann David Wyss*, **Robinson Crusoe** *by Daniel Defoe*, **The Count of Monte Cristo**
s Family Robinson by Johann David Wyss, **The Adventures of Pinocchio** *by Carlo Collodi* and **Twenty Thousand Leagues Under the Sea** *by Jules Verne* ✧ THE HOLE ✧ **Alice's Adventures in Wonderland** *by Lewis Carroll* ✧*